Rookie
reader

BUBBLE TROUBLE

By Joy N. Hulme
Illustrated by Mike Cressy

Children's Press®
A Division of Scholastic Inc.
New York Toronto London Auckland Sydney
Mexico City New Delhi Hong Kong
Danbury, Connecticut

For all my bubble-blowing buddies
—J. N. H.

To Dolly Bentas Cressy, protector and muse
—M. C.

Reading Consultant
Linda Cornwell
Learning Resource Consultant
Indiana Department of Education

Library of Congress Cataloging-in-Publication Data
Hulme, Joy N.
    Bubble trouble / by Joy N. Hulme ; illustrated by Mike Cressy.
        p. cm. — (Rookie reader)
    Summary: Bubbles grow and flow, fly in the sky, and pop, but dipping the stick
and blowing can make more.
    ISBN 0-516-21584-1 (lib.bdg.)   0-516-26473-7 (pbk.)
    [1. Bubbles—Fiction. 2. Stories in rhyme.] I. Cressy, Mike, ill. II. Title. III. Series.
PZ8.3.H878Bu   1999
[E]—dc21
                                                                        98-8056
                                                                          CIP
                                                                          AC

12 13 14 15 R 08 07   62

Dip the stick in bubble stuff,

give a slow and steady puff.

Oh! Oh!

See them grow.

7

How they flow,

and glow and go,

fast

and slow.

Watch them fly
in the sky,

low

and high.

Oh, oh, bubble trouble.

Stop! Stop! Don't pop!

21

No, no, not that!

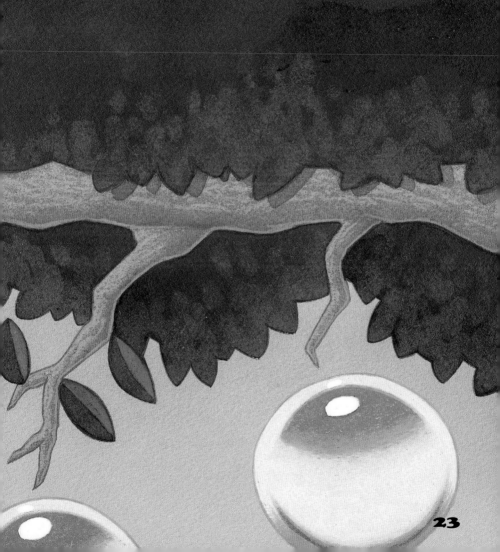

SPLAT!

Do not sigh,

do not cry.

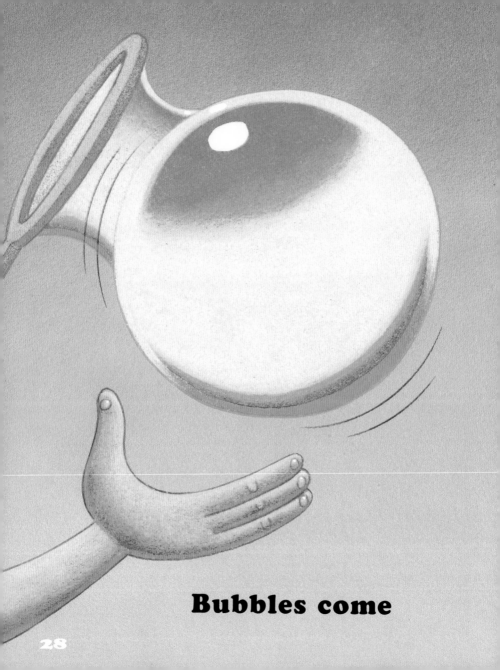

Bubbles come

and bubbles go.

Dip the stick again and blow.

Word List (42 words)

a	fast	no	stick
again	flow	not	stop
and	fly	oh	stuff
blow	give	pop	that
bubble	glow	puff	the
bubbles	go	see	them
come	grow	sigh	they
cry	high	sky	trouble
dip	how	slow	watch
do	in	splat	
don't	low	steady	

About the Author

Joy N. Hulme, author of thirteen books, describes herself as a grandma with the heart of a child. Growing up in Utah, she was rich in all the things a youngster needs: loving parents, siblings and cousins to play with, woods to wander in, farm fields to explore, trees to climb, rocks, logs and adobe bricks to build with, and a huge lawn for tumbling.

Still in love with nature, Joy lives in California with her husband, Mel. She delights in blowing bubbles, especially the giant-size variety, with her children, grandchildren, and her fun and faithful friend, Elizabeth.

About the Illustrator

Mike Cressy resides in the rainiest part of the United States, paints pictures, and tries to stay warm and dry in his hovel, with the help of some hot cocoa.